Get in the Game! With Robin Roberts

BASKETBALL YEAR

WHAT IT'S LIKE TO BE A WOMAN PRO

The Millbrook Press
Brookfield, Connecticut

The author and publisher wish to thank Bill Gutman for his research and writing contributions to this series.

Published by The Millbrook Press, Inc.
2 Old New Milford Road
Brookfield, Connecticut 06804
www.millbrookpress.com

Cover photographs courtesy of Steve Fenn/ABC and Duomo (© 1997 William Sallaz). Photographs courtesy of AP/Wide World Photos: pp. 6, 9 (bottom), 10-11, 43, 44; UPI/Corbis-Bettmann: p. 9 (top); WNBA Enterprises: pp. 13 (© Fernando Medina), 15 (center © Fernando Medina), 27 (© Andrew D. Bernstein), 32 (© Gary Bassing), 40 (© Rob Bean); Duomo: pp. 15 (top © 1996 William R. Sallaz; bottom © 1997 Darren Carroll), 23 (© 1997 William R. Sallaz), 25 (© 1997 Chris Trotman); © Michelle V. Agins: pp. 17, 19, 20; Allsport: p. 28 (© Ezra O. Shaw); Houston Chronicle: p. 33; John Atashian: p. 35; © Phaedra Singelis: p. 36; Airc Crabb: p. 37; Liaison Agency: p. 41 (© Pam Francis)

Library of Congress Cataloging-in-Publication Data
Roberts, Robin, 1960–
Basketball year : what it's like to be a woman pro.
p. cm. — (Get in the game! With Robin Roberts)
Includes bibliographical references and index.
Summary: Describes various aspects of being a woman who plays professional basketball: training, travel, game play, interacting with fans, and everyday life.
ISBN 0-7613-1406-7 (lib. bdg.) —ISBN 0-7613-1028-2 (pbk.)
1. Basketball for women—Vocational guidance—United States—Juvenile literature. 2. Women basketball players—United States—Juvenile literature. [1. Basketball for women. 2. Women basketball players.] I. Title.
GV886 .R62 2000 796.323'02373—dc21 99-046223

CONTENTS

Introduction

Sports has always been a big part of my life. From playing sandlot football with the other kids in my neighborhood in Biloxi, Mississippi, to playing tennis in high school and basketball in college, to working in sports broadcasting at ESPN, I can't imagine my life without sports. It used to be that girls who played sports were labeled "tomboys." These days, however, women and sports go hand-in-hand in so many ways.

Sports can increase a girl's confidence and help her to feel good about herself, and can help her succeed in nearly every aspect of life including school, a career, and relationships with friends and family.

With **Get in the Game!** my goal is to share my love and knowledge of the world of sports, and to show just how important sports can be. What you can learn on the field, court, rink, and arena are ways to solve problems, communicate with others, and become a leader. No matter what your skill level, if you learn all that sports can teach you, how can you *not* succeed at life in general? And the best part is that, like I have, you'll have fun at the same time!

—Robin Roberts

All-Star Lisa Leslie of the Los Angeles Sparks moves the ball in the very first WNBA All-Star Game, held in July 1999. Leslie's team, the Western Conference, won 79-61, and she was named Most Valuable Player of the game.

1 PROS At Last

What is it like to be a professional basketball player? If you are a woman, there was no way to really know until 1996. Up to that time, no professional women's basketball league had been successful in the United States. Then, suddenly, there were two. The American Basketball League (ABL) began playing in October 1996, and the Women's National Basketball Association (WNBA) swung into action in June 1997.

For the first time, America's finest female basketball players didn't have to go to Europe, Asia, or other foreign places to be paid for playing a game they love. Finally, they would be paid professionals playing before cheering fans in their own country—a country where the sport of basketball had been invented more than a hundred years earlier. For women, this opportunity had surely been a long time coming.

Though basketball was created as a sport for both men and women, in the early years women played a very different game of basketball than men. In some ways, the rules of the women's game kept them from developing the many skills needed to play well. Women were restricted to certain zones on the court that they could not leave. They were allowed just a single dribble before the rules required them to make a pass. And unlike the men's game, in which there are five players to a side, there were six players to a side: three forwards and three guards, with only the forwards allowed to score.

It wasn't until the 1971-1972 season that the women's collegiate game finally resembled the men's. That meant full-court basketball with five players to a side, unlimited dribbling, and 30 seconds to make a shot.

With these modified rules, the women's skills developed. In fact, a succession of outstanding women players came out of the college ranks in the 1970s and 1980s. These women could play for the United States National Team, which competed in the world championships and a few other events. They could also try out for the United States Olympic team, which competed every four years. But the only place they could play basketball for pay as professionals was overseas.

By the middle of the 1990s, women's college basketball was more popular and successful than ever. The time seemed right to create a professional basketball league for women. Some of the top players were making good money playing overseas. What they really wanted, however, was to showcase their talents in front of American fans. Cynthia Cooper, who would become the first-ever Most Valuable Player (MVP) in the WNBA, played in Spain

Women's hoops has come a long way since this picture was taken of a high school team in 1923. Back then, it was a slower game that didn't give players many chances to develop their skills.

Rebecca Lobo, now of the New York Liberty, pulls in a rebound during a 1995 game her college team, the Connecticut Huskies, played against the Tennessee Lady Vols. Great college teams like these made women's basketball popular and helped pave the way for the formation of a professional league.

and Italy for 11 years. She described what was missing from her career in a single sentence: "I could score 60 points in a game and I'd still come home to a telephone," she said.

In other words, no one from home was there to watch her great performances. Another American star, Dawn Staley from the University of Virginia, voiced similar feelings about her stay overseas. "A lot of money went toward phone bills and bringing people over to keep me company," she said. "The only reason I played overseas was to get the international experience to help me make the U.S. National Team. Overseas was my sacrifice. Playing as a pro in the United States will be my reward."

That's what all the top players wanted in the 1990s—a chance to play at home. Sheryl Swoopes, who scored an incredible 47 points for

Texas Tech in their championship victory over Ohio State in 1993, said the women had always been envious of the men. "We would sit home and watch the [NBA] draft," Swoopes said, "and we'd see the men getting their caps . . . when they knew what team they were

WNBA players
model their teams' uniforms
before the start of the first
WNBA season in 1997.

year, but both had the same goal: to put talented teams on the court and build a fan base for a brand-new professional sport. The players would have to do more than just shoot three-pointers and play defense. They also had to become nearly full-time spokespersons for their sport.

Being a pro takes a great deal of effort both on and off the court. Although the season may last just a few months, being a pro is a year-round job. So what *is* it like to be a woman professional basketball player? The pros themselves can finally show us.

going to. All we wanted was the same opportunity."

With the creation of the ABL and the WNBA, that opportunity came. The top female players were now professionals. The two leagues operated a bit differently and their seasons were at different times of the

2 The PRE-Season

Every woman playing professional basketball loves the game and cherishes the idea that she is now a professional athlete. It's the chance she always wanted. Yet none thought the life of a pro would be easy. There would be hard work both on and off the court. The newest professionals soon learned what other pros have known for years: To be at the top of your game, you have to work at it for nearly 12 months of the year.

The two professional leagues that were created, the ABL and the WNBA (the ABL disbanded in 1998), had different seasons, but the players' experiences were very similar. For that reason, examples from both leagues are used.

There are not a lot of openings for a woman professional basketball player, and competition is tough. If a player doesn't work as hard as she can, she may find herself out of a job, since there are so many others capable of replacing her. The pre-season is one of the most important times for a player to do her best.

Personal appearances, whether they are school visits or charitable events, always include autograph-signing sessions, like this one in which Nikki McCray of the Washington Mystics is participating.

PUBLIC RELATIONS

Because the league is working to build a fan base and good community relations, the first month of the pre-season is used mostly for promotional work. Players who spend the rest of the year elsewhere get settled in their team's city, and all the players deal with a huge volume of public relations.

Every day of the month, players will make one to three personal appearances within their communities. These may include speaking to elementary school classes, attending high school rallies, or taking part in a variety of community events. Some of these can be weekend fairs and fund-raising programs. As Pam Batalis, the former vice president of sales for the ABL, explained, introducing the players to the community is an important goal. "We want all the people, and especially young girls, to see that the players are real people, someone that young girls can become," she said.

Also during this first month, the players take physical exams and complete their public relations paperwork. This includes having their photos taken for the media guides and other publications, and meeting with the media relations department of their team to supply their biographies and other personal information that will be made available to local and national media. Players who don't live in their team's city year-round must also look for housing during this period, so that everything is set by the time training camp begins.

The players must also work out regularly during this first month. They will meet with their team's strength and conditioning coach, who will map out a weight program for them, and they will play many pickup games, often against local men's teams.

TRAINING CAMP

Once players are in training camp and begin practicing, they have very little free time. Training camp schedules are so grueling that only top athletes will be able to complete them.

Strength training is an important part of a player's conditioning. Nikki McCray (front) and three-time Olympic gold medalist and former ABL star Teresa Edwards work out together during the 1996 Olympic games as members of Team USA.

Training camp is tough! Nykesha Sales of the Orlando Miracle flies up the court during an intense practice game.

For an athlete, there's no such thing as too much stretching, and Sheryl Swoopes of the Houston Comets does her share.

"Training camp is horrible," said Lori Montgomery, media relations director of the Cleveland Rockers. "For fourteen straight days the team has two-a-day workouts. The first is from 9 A.M. to 1 P.M., the second from 5 P.M. to 6 P.M. After the morning workout, the players do their weight lifting, then spend an hour in the locker room watching tapes and going over plays."

Even when practices are reduced to once a day, it doesn't get much easier. For example, the Cleveland Rockers will practice from 9 A.M. until noon. But following that, there are locker room sessions, organized stretching, and then scrimmages (practice games) in the evening. One thing all teams seem to have in common is that these scrimmages are usually against men's teams.

"We bring in a lot of division 1 college graduates," said Montgomery. "These are topflight men's players. Our theory is that the girls can get soft playing against each other. It's really great for the girls to go up against the men. The play gets really physical and the girls get roughed up a little. That's good for them."

Missy Bequette, who coached an ABL team, voiced similar thoughts. "Guys are physically stronger and very competitive. Having our club play alongside and against men gives them a great chance to work on various aspects of their game and with no pressure."

Finally, the pre-season is a time for the players to come together as a team. They spend a great deal of time together at dinners and other group activities. As Bequette put it, "We want to make it a bonding situation. The players are going to be spending . . . months together and we want them as close as possible."

The time spent in the pre-season bonding as a team helps to keep the players close all season—and a group hug before a game, such as this one demonstrated by the Liberty, doesn't hurt, either.

The pre-season is a time to get teams ready. As with any professional sports team, that means a great deal of hard work. Not only must the players get in tip-top physical condition, they must hone their individual basketball skills and learn to mesh as a team. In addition, they must establish good work habits for the upcoming season.

What makes women's pro basketball different from other pro sports is its newness. The players know they may only get one chance to make the league work. Everyone involved knows she needs to make an extra effort to establish a good relationship with the fans. The pre-season is an important time to work on this, as well. Getting to know and establish a bond with the fans is not only something all players are required to do, it is something they *want* to do.

3 The REGULAR Season

Just the basketball part of the regular season is enough to keep the players busy. They must prepare for games, play the games, and take care of their bodies in between by continually working with coaches and trainers to keep in tip-top physical shape. But there is much more to the season than basketball. The job of a woman professional basketball player doesn't begin and end when the whistle blows. The women must be prepared to handle all the various elements that go into the season.

TRAVELING

Going on the road is a part of life for every professional sports team. It means playing in other cities in front of opposing fans, living in hotels, and often being away from loved ones. For the women pros, traveling is a little more difficult than it is for the men. Because the women's salaries and travel budgets are not as high as in men's sports, the women have to do more for them-selves.

Woman players, for example, fly commercial airlines rather than char-

Teresa Weatherspoon, known simply as "Spoon," uses some bus travel time to motivate her New York Liberty teammates.

tered team planes, as the men do. The women are responsible for getting themselves to the airport in most cases, often carpooling to make it easier. Coast-to-coast plane trips can be tiring, and players usually do what most airline passengers do—sleep, read, watch a movie, listen to CDs, or grab the ear of a teammate and talk.

Once they reach their destination, players generally go to a hotel

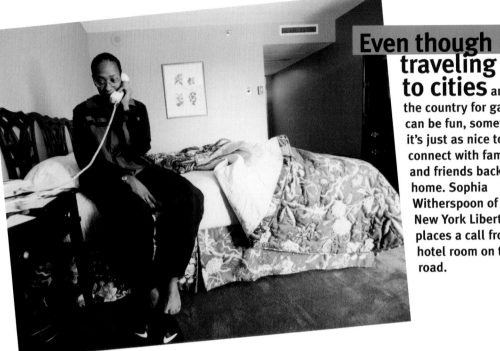

Even though traveling to cities around the country for games can be fun, sometimes it's just as nice to connect with family and friends back home. Sophia Witherspoon of the New York Liberty places a call from her hotel room on the road.

near the arena where they will be playing. Players double-up, two in a room, and rotate roommates on road trips. That way, each player always has a different roommate. This helps them get to know their teammates better and helps prevent the formation of cliques, which can affect the team's play.

Since there are some women pros who are married, however, and a few who have children, the teams make some special allowances. Children and husbands are allowed to travel with the team, but must pay their own way. If a family wants to stay together in a hotel, they must pay the difference in price of the double room paid for by the team and the private room they wish to use.

The reason for these arrangements is that team budgets are not nearly as high as those of men's sports. And the players don't have multimillion-dollar contracts with all kinds of provisions that make them pampered athletes, as is often the case with the men. So if the women players want anything extra, they must pay for it themselves.

Traveling doesn't allow the players much spare time. If the team's hotel is close to a mall, players might use a free afternoon to go shopping. If they arrive in town the night before the game and have friends in that city, they can visit. But there is surprisingly little time for sightseeing. A player may visit a city four or five times and only know the immediate area around the hotel and arena.

Game days on the road usually begin with players having an easy shoot-around in the morning, just to get the basketball muscles loose. Then they may take the afternoon off before bussing to the arena as a team. Depending on its schedule, the team may fly out after the game or the next morning. If they are to leave the next morning, players often visit with friends or with players from the home team, take in a movie, or go to a restaurant after a game. Since most are tired from the game, and since flights are generally scheduled early, it's rarely a late night out.

"Travel is rough, very wearing," confirmed Lori Montgomery. "The longer trips, especially those to other time zones, can really take a lot out of the players. They have to be concerned all the time about their conditioning.

"Even after a horrible day of travel, the girls have to go to the gym to shoot around, or find a pool for a workout, something to get all the different muscles working. This is something they have to think about constantly when they're on the road."

PLAYING AT HOME

Sometimes it seems that the best thing about going on the road is that the team will eventually come home. In their home cities, the players have their own apartments and those who are married or who have children generally live with their families. But even when the team is home for a stretch of several days, there still isn't a lot of free time.

Perhaps it is those few players with children who have the most hectic home schedule. Former coach Missy Bequette confirmed that. "A player with a child or children must be more organized than the others. Not only does she have all the responsibilities that go with the team, but she has to make sure her children get to and from school, find the right people to watch them when necessary, and keep a tab on their activities from week to week. It's a lot to do."

The players without children, however, also have a busy schedule when the team is home. "If players have a free day at home," Lori Montgomery explains, "they try to do the things any other person would do—go grocery shopping, pay bills, take clothes to the dry cleaners. That sounds almost normal, but

Sheryl Swoopes spends a moment with her son, Jordan, during the 1997 WNBA championships. Swoopes missed the beginning of the WNBA's first season because of her pregnancy, but joined her team, the Houston Comets, just in time to help it win the championship.

it has to be squeezed in between a lot of other things."

Those other things revolve totally around basketball. Players have to continue to work at home throughout the season to keep themselves in shape and as healthy as possible. A rare day off often means a session with the trainer, dealing with minor injuries and perhaps mapping out a rehabilitation program that can be carried out while the player travels and competes.

For the women, playing basketball at the home court means much more than just going out on the floor and trying to beat the opponent. During the entire season, each and every player goes above and beyond shooting, dribbling, scoring, and defending. Part of a pro's life in the women's game is interacting with the fans in ways that haven't been seen in professional sports in years. At home every team has comprehensive and time-consuming programs that allow fans the closest interaction with players of any major sports league. This kind of fan interaction plays a huge role in every player's life.

Shana Daum, former media relations director for an ABL team, explained the way the players approach the fans. The players "become involved in public relations work as soon as they come to town before training camp. But we continue it throughout the season. There are designated players sent out to sign autographs after each game. As tired as they are, players often come out on their own, when it isn't even their turn. They simply want to do it."

Certain games are designated as "fan club" games. That gives all fans

Lisa Leslie signs
**autographs for a swarm of
admirers before a game in 1997.**

who are official members of a
team's fan club a chance to gather
after a game and interact with the
team's coaches and one or two players. Each player must participate in
one of these sessions during the
season.

Public relations director for the
Washington Mystics, Julie Demeo,
backed that up. "There are autograph sessions after every game—
win or lose. No matter what, two of
our players must go out there, smile,
talk to fans, and sign autographs

despite how they feel about the game. The players know they have to do it because the fans are the cornerstone of the WNBA.

"We don't want our players to become untouchable icons, something that has happened too often in men's sports. Our players know part of their job is to bring fans to the league. All the women in the league are gracious to the fans. They turn to fans, create relationships, and enjoy being associated with the community. This is a big part of their daily job."

Many of the players interact with fans on their own, showing again that they appreciate being pros and really want to keep the fans coming. Vicky Bullett of the Charlotte Sting was doing a postgame autograph session when it appeared she had finally finished.

But instead of turning and walking away, Bullett asked loudly, "Have I missed anyone?"

Michele Timms, an Australian star who plays for the Phoenix Mercury, spent two hours signing autographs after the team's very first home opener. When she finally had to leave, there were still people waiting. Timms then wrote a letter to the *Arizona Republic* newspaper in which she apologized for not being able to stay to sign for each and every person who was there.

During a fan appreciation night at Madison Square Garden, a young fan yelled to the New York Liberty's star point guard Teresa Weatherspoon that she was her hero. Spoon immediately dropped what she was doing, ran into the stands, and gave the young girl a big hug.

Michele Timms
of the Phoenix Mercury places a great deal of importance on interaction with the fans, as she demonstrated after her team's very first game.

THE GAME

All the promotion in the world will mean very little unless there is a solid product behind it. Being ready to play and then giving their best on the court still remains the number one priority of all the players in women's pro basketball. That means thinking about the game every single day, practicing hard at all times, keeping fit and strong, and working to improve all individual phases of the game. It's a tall order for any athlete.

Teresa Weatherspoon (#11), loves tigers. "I love their mentality and I try to carry that," she said. "If you look at a tiger's attack, they spring up on you and that's what I think I do. A tiger protects his territory, and I feel like I have to protect my territory."

Women's basketball emphasizes a strong team game, with sharp passing, a lot of running, and tight defense. The scores aren't as high as those in the NBA, but many of the women's games are close. Every player has to be ready to go hard whenever she is on the court.

There are great players with outstanding individual skills. Houston's Cynthia Cooper has been called the WNBA version of Michael Jordan, thanks to her ability to take over a game at crunch time. Washington's Nikki McCray loves to drive hard to the basket. Teresa Weatherspoon would rather disrupt the opposition with great defense or a key steal than anything else. The Detroit Shock's Jennifer Azzi is capable of winning a game with clutch shooting. Sheryl Swoopes is an all-around player who excels at every phase of the game, while Dawn Staley of the

Charlotte Sting is a point guard who can excite a crowd with her pinpoint passing, showstopping fakes, and behind-the-back assists.

Though the women's season is not nearly as long as the NBA's 82-game schedule, there are some times that are tougher than others. Like other athletes, the women of pro basketball must be prepared for these difficult parts of their season.

"The toughest part for the players is to stay motivated throughout the entire year," said Bequette. "Usually mid-season is the most difficult time of year for the players. Other teams know your strengths by then and are playing you tougher. And the little injuries are beginning to build up.

"[The mid-season] can also be difficult for those who don't get a lot of playing time. Everyone was a star in high school, and maybe in college. Now those who are bench players must adjust. They have to stay motivated and keep working hard if they want to play more."

The Washington Mystics joined the WNBA as an expansion team and won just three games in their first season. Staying motivated was a special challenge for them. "Many of our players came from winning programs," said Julie Demeo. "They don't like to lose. I think they found [the pro level] a lot more competitive and had to adjust. Smaller players also had to adjust, as did players learning a new position. A center in college might be playing forward in the pros. These are things our players had to concentrate on and work at each and every day."

During the season there is little free time for a professional basketball player. Playing, winning traveling, promoting, staying fit— these are the things the players think about most.

"The girls do not really have time for a social life during the season," explained Shana Daum. "Most of them are very private about their lives. They get calls asking if they are married or have boyfriends. But during the season it is usually 'thanks, but no thanks.' These are just some of the sacrifices they have to make as professionals."

As every woman pro would probably agree, it's more than a full-time job. During the season, it's practically a player's whole life.

4 *The* OFF-Season

There was a time in professional sports when the "off" season was just that. Once the season ended, players did something else until the next season began. Years ago, that might have meant simply getting another job, since most sports salaries were very low. But times have changed.

In men's sports, the money is now so good that players can do whatever they want in the off-season. A big part of that is usually staying in shape for the following season. But most women do not make the same kind of money. For them, the off-season must be productive in several ways.

STAYING IN SHAPE

When the season ends, basketball doesn't stop. All teams give their players a final evaluation. The coaches will point out to each player the phases of her game that need to be improved, whether it's ball handling, defense, or long-

Wendy Palmer of the Detroit Shock
enjoys teaching kids about the game she loves at recreational
programs held during the off-season.

range shooting. A player might be told to spend more time in the weight room to improve her strength. In any case, the player must do this on her own, in addition to the other off-season activities she is pursuing.

Because the WNBA season is rather short, some players decide to use the off-season to play overseas, and are free to make their own contractual deals.

"A lot of the girls are still going [to play in foreign countries]," said Lori Montgomery. "Some do it strictly for the extra money. In fact, some of the veterans can still make a hundred thousand dollars for a short European season, more than they make here. Others go for the opportunity to play and improve their games. I don't think anyone loves it, but the option is still there. If it [the WNBA] expands to a four- or five-month season instead of three, then I think you'll see it stop."

The European seasons are shorter and physically easier on the players, who practice perhaps twice a week. Veteran player Janice Braxton of the Rockers, at age 36, had also played in Italy for 14 years. In addition, she had negotiated an arrangement in which she didn't have to practice between games. For her, playing overseas was a way to keep her skills sharp without wearing her body down. Plus she was well paid for her services.

Younger players who haven't been overseas may go for the experi-

Cynthia Cooper cools down after doing double-duty at an off-season 5-K run. Running helps to keep her in shape, and money raised by the run benefits cancer research. Coop wore number 10 to remember her teammate and friend Kim Perrott, who had died of cancer a few months earlier.

ence. Knowing they have a league to return to, they view it more as a learning experience, a chance to see another country and to play against different, veteran players.

According to Montgomery, even those who don't go to Europe in the off-season view basketball as a full-time job. Some coach high school or college teams and stay in shape by working out with their respective teams. Others play in pickup games, often with and against men. Almost all of the women run to keep in shape, and follow the exercise regimen that their trainers have laid out for them.

If a player lives full time in the city where she plays, then she may be called upon to make some personal appearances or do some interviews on behalf of her team in the off-season. "It's almost like an

unstated obligation," explained Shana Daum. "Players don't mind coming in during the off-season."

Daum said that players often check in with their team once a week during the off-season, reporting on their training programs and talking about their progress on the court.

Similarly, Missy Bequette noted, "Players are given a list of [basketball] things to work on so they'll come back better players," she said. "They know they have to work hard, keep their conditioning and their strength. Most of them will find pickup games against good competition and will play throughout the off-season."

LIFE OUTSIDE BASKETBALL

Players also stay busy in matters away from the court and the team. Some return to school to work

Rebecca Lobo brushed up on her
**broadcasting skills by co-commentating on the National
Collegiate Athletics Association (NCAA) women's
basketball tournament. Here we are in the ESPN studios.**

toward a college degree or an
advanced degree. Others go to work
in a variety of jobs and professions.
Some of these women were working
at other careers before the pro
leagues began. Others pursue alter-
nate careers because they are
already looking to the day when
their basketball careers will end. But
no matter what they are doing, basketball is not very far away.

Rebecca Lobo of the New York
Liberty is considering a broadcasting
career and has worked as a com-
mentator at college games during
her off-season.

Among other things, Sheryl Swoopes is involved in writing books for children.

The Cleveland Rockers' Suzie McConnell-Serio, a mother of four, coaches high school basketball, something she did before coming out of retirement to play in the WNBA.

Jennifer Azzi, of the Detroit Shock, runs two basketball camps during the off-season which emphasize giving back to the community as

Suzie McConnell-Serio is one of the players who balances her family responsibilities with her basketball career. In addition to playing a full schedule during the season and coaching high school basketball during the off-season, she is a mother to four small Cleveland Rockers fans.

Jennifer Azzi talks to a group of aspiring WNBA-ers during her 1999 off-season basketball camp.

well as teaching the sport. Clarisse Machanguana of the Los Angeles Sparks has studied pre-law, while Sonja Henning, who earned a law degree before coming back to play in the ABL (she now plays for the WNBA Houston Comets), works several days a week at a law firm during the off-season.

Murriel Page of the Washington Mystics returned to the University of Florida, and her teammate, Rita Williams, to the University of Connecticut to finish their degrees.

Other players take the time to work with sponsors or companies that have given them endorsement deals. The off-season is often the

best time to work with the companies on advertising campaigns.

While the off-season gives players an opportunity to pursue other interests, take care of business other than basketball, spend time with families, or look into second careers, basketball is never an afterthought. All find the time to work on their game, their conditioning, and to represent their team and their sport. The players know that they are building something for the future and are willing to make a commitment to that. The next season is never very far off.

5 The Responsibility of Being a PRO

The women of professional basketball know that young girls are watching them and looking up to them as role models. Sheryl Swoopes remembers how it was before there was a professional league for women. "We had to watch little girls looking for basketball role models and asking their parents to buy them jerseys with [Michael] Jordan and [Charles] Barkley and [Grant] Hill on them," Swoopes said. "I understand the popularity of the NBA players, but it hurt a little bit that we did not have the opportunity to be role models for little girls with dreams of playing professional basketball. Now I think we have that chance."

Being role models and relating to the fans is a responsibility that all the players have taken to heart. Shana Daum said that, in a sense, the women give up some of their privacy to be role models for young girls. "[The players] are very cognizant of their behavior," she said. "When they're out in public, people know who they are. Some of the

The women pros take their role-model status very seriously, and want to use their popularity to encourage their young fans, especially the girls, to set goals and work toward achieving them.

players have told me they've been in restaurants and were going to order a drink or a beer. Then they see a little girl pointing to them and think twice about having the drink. Being a role model does involve some sacrifice."

"Being accessible to fans is the cornerstone of the league," said Lori Montgomery. "The players are pioneers working to build a new league, so their job becomes bringing fans

into the building. The players show great emotion on the floor, but win or lose, always remain gracious to the fans. They go out of their way to create relationships."

Pam Batalis says that the majority of the players are naturals at fostering good public relations with the fans and winning new friends for the sport. "The players are used to crowds and are intelligent, personable people," Batalis said. "Most are . . . well-educated and articulate. They take their public relations responsibility very seriously."

Cultivating relationships with fans is not the only responsibility women pros have undertaken. Women's issues have also become very important. During the first WNBA season, it was revealed that two of its highest-profile players—Houston's Cynthia Cooper and New York's Rebecca Lobo—were both helping their mothers battle breast cancer. That led to the entire league getting into the fight.

General Motors Corporation became involved. They signed a multiyear agreement with Cooper that had the league's Most Valuable Player join fellow stars Lobo and Lisa Leslie of the Los Angeles Sparks as GM spokespersons to help promote GM brands and its Concept:Cure program—an effort designed to help a variety of worthy causes, including the fight against breast cancer.

"The one thing I've had all my life," said Cynthia Cooper, "is this fire that burns inside of me, that says I can do it, I can accomplish anything I've set my mind to. I get it from my mother, and I never let anyone put out that fire." Coop's mom has since passed away.

Other women joined the fight, using their public forum as professional athletes to draw more attention to a cause that can benefit many.

In addition, many players help favorite local or personal charities, or programs benefitting the needy. They do this as part of their team's community involvement and, in many cases, on their own. Jennifer Azzi's basketball camps were an example.

"The camp chose one organization to help," explained Shana Daum. "It was a homeless shelter in San Jose. Jennifer herself made a cash contribution on behalf of the campers, and the kids brought in canned goods and clothes to donate to the shelter. It's all part of the responsibility of being a pro, and remembering those who support you."

Another responsibility is that felt by the older players to the youngsters coming into the pros from college. The veterans remember what it was like not to have a professional opportunity in their own country. They want to be sure that the new players don't feel that they automatically have it made.

"We've encouraged our older players to share their experiences with the younger ones," said Pam Batalis. "We want them to know what it was like playing in Europe, being lonely, and not having a league to call their own. That way, [the younger players] will hopefully appreciate what they have, not take it for granted, and work to make it stronger."

The veteran players take the responsibility of letting the younger players know how it was and how lucky they are. They want to teach appreciation and reinforce that the

Chamique Holdsclaw (left), of the Washington Mystics, a rookie in the 1999 season, represents the future of the WNBA, while her defender, Sheryl Swoopes (right), is part of the old guard who remembers what it was like before there was a professional league. The two are pictured during the inaugural WNBA All-Star Game in 1999.

Teamwork, dedication to the sport of basketball, serving as ambassadors to adoring fans, and building for the future of women's sports—these responsibilities and more make up a year in the life of a WNBA player.

opportunities available as a woman pro basketball player are unique and should be taken seriously.

Being a pro in the WNBA means a lot more than making baskets, getting rebounds, and putting wins on the scoreboard. Winning might be the bottom line in any sport, but professional basketball for women has proven to be more than that.

Responsibility extends far beyond the playing court. It moves out into the communities where the players are looked upon as a whole new group of heroes. A pro is a pro for all 12 months of the year. The hardworking players know that it's very important to the future of the women's game that their images remain as high as their personal and team goals.

Get in the Game!

The official Web site of the WNBA has lots of great information and is easy to navigate. You can find it at WNBA.com, of course! There are also many books that will give you a glimpse into the lives of the pros, as well as into the WNBA, and basketball in general. Players and team rosters are changing all the time, but most books are good sources of basic information. A few are listed below.

Inside the WNBA: A Behind-the-Scenes Photo Scrapbook by Joe Layden and James Preller, with an introduction by WNBA President Val Ackerman (New York: Scholastic, 1999).

Teresa Weatherspoon's Basketball for Girls by Teresa Weatherspoon and Kelly Whiteside (New York: John Wiley & Sons, 1999).

The Best of the Best in Basketball by Rachel Rutledge, Women of Sports Series (Brookfield, CT: Millbrook, 1998).

She's Got Game: 10 Stars of the WNBA by Michelle Smith (New York: Scholastic, 1999).

Teamwork: The Charlotte Sting in Action by Tom Owens and Diana Star Helmer (New York: PowerKids Press, 1999). This series also includes books about the Cleveland Rockers, Houston Comets, Los Angeles Sparks, New York Liberty, Phoenix Mercury, and Sacramento Monarchs.

Index